PRAISE FOR M. L. BUCHMAN

Tom Clancy fans open to a strong female lead will clamor for more.

— *DRONE*, PUBLISHERS WEEKLY

Superb! Miranda is utterly compelling!

— *BOOKLIST*, STARRED REVIEW

Escape Rating: A. Five Stars! OMG just start with *Drone* and be prepared for a fantastic binge-read!

— READING REALITY, MIRANDA CHASE SERIES

The best military thriller I've read in a very long time. Love the female characters.

— *DRONE*, SHELDON MCARTHUR, FOUNDER OF THE MYSTERY BOOKSTORE, LA

Meticulously researched, hard-hitting, and suspenseful.

— *PURE HEAT*, PUBLISHERS WEEKLY, STARRED REVIEW

A fabulous soaring thriller.

— *TAKE OVER AT MIDNIGHT,* MIDWEST
BOOK REVIEW

Buchman has catapulted his way to the top tier of my
favorite authors.

— FRESH FICTION

Nonstop action that will keep readers on the edge of
their seats.

— *TAKE OVER AT MIDNIGHT,* LIBRARY
JOURNAL

M L. Buchman's ability to keep the reader right in
the middle of the action is amazing.

— LONG AND SHORT REVIEWS

The only thing you'll ask yourself is, "When does the
next one come out?"

— *WAIT UNTIL MIDNIGHT,* RT REVIEWS, 4
STARS

I knew the books would be good, but I didn't realize
how good.

— NIGHT STALKERS SERIES, KIRKUS
REVIEWS

ICED CHEF

A KATE STARK THRILLER SHORT STORY

M. L. BUCHMAN

SIGN UP FOR M. L. BUCHMAN'S NEWSLETTER TODAY

and receive:
Release News
Free Short Stories
a Free Book

Get your free book today. Do it now.
free-book.mlbuchman.com

Other works by M. L. Buchman: (* - also in audio)

Action-Adventure Thrillers

Kate Stark
Final Taste
Ice Burn
Knife's Edge

Miranda Chase
*Drone**
*Thunderbolt**
*Condor**
*Ghostrider**
*Raider**
*Chinook**
*Havoc**
*White Top**
*Start the Chase**
*Lightning**
*Skibird**
*Nightwatch**
*Osprey**
*Gryphon**
*Wedgetail**

Science Fiction / Fantasy

Deities Anonymous
Cookbook from Hell: Reheated
Saviors 101

Contemporary Romance

Eagle Cove
Return to Eagle Cove
Recipe for Eagle Cove
Longing for Eagle Cove
Keepsake for Eagle Cove

Love Abroad
Heart of the Cotswolds: England
Path of Love: Cinque Terre, Italy

Where Dreams
Where Dreams are Born
Where Dreams Reside
*Where Dreams Are of Christmas**
Where Dreams Unfold
Where Dreams Are Written
Where Dreams Continue

Non-Fiction

Strategies for Success
Managing Your Inner Artist/Writer
*Estate Planning for Authors**
Character Voice
*Narrate and Record Your Own Audiobook**
Beyond Prince Charming: One Guy's Guide to Writing Men in Romance

Short Story Series by M. L. Buchman:

Action-Adventure Thrillers

Kate Stark
Miranda Chase Stories

Romantic Suspense

Antarctic Ice Fliers
US Coast Guard

Contemporary Romance

Eagle Cove

Other

Deities Anonymous (fantasy)
Single Titles

The Emily Beale Universe
(military romantic suspense)

The Night Stalkers
MAIN FLIGHT
The Night Is Mine
I Own the Dawn
Wait Until Dark
Take Over at Midnight
Light Up the Night
Bring On the Dusk
By Break of Day
Target of the Heart
Target Lock on Love
Target of Mine
Target of One's Own
NIGHT STALKERS HOLIDAYS
Daniel's Christmas*
Frank's Independence Day*
Peter's Christmas*
Christmas at Steel Beach
Zachary's Christmas*
Roy's Independence Day*
Damien's Christmas*
Christmas at Peleliu Cove

Henderson's Ranch
Nathan's Big Sky*
Big Sky, Loyal Heart*
Big Sky Dog Whisperer*
Tales of Henderson's Ranch*

Shadow Force: Psi
At the Slightest Sound*
At the Quietest Word*
At the Merest Glance*
At the Clearest Sensation*

White House Protection Force
Off the Leash*
On Your Mark*
In the Weeds*

Firehawks
Pure Heat
Full Blaze
Hot Point*
Flash of Fire*
Wild Fire
SMOKEJUMPERS
Wildfire at Dawn*
Wildfire at Larch Creek*
Wildfire on the Skagit*

Delta Force
Target Engaged*
Heart Strike*
Wild Justice*
Midnight Trust*

Night Stalkers Reload
Guard the East Flank*

Emily Beale Universe Short Story Series

The Night Stalkers
The Night Stalkers Stories
The Night Stalkers CSAR
The Night Stalkers Wedding Stories
The Future Night Stalkers

Delta Force
Th Delta Force Shooters
The Delta Force Warriors

Firehawks
The Firehawks Lookouts
The Firehawks Hotshots
The Firebirds

White House Protection Force
Stories

Future Night Stalkers
Stories (Science Fiction)

ABOUT THIS BOOK

WHEN ICE-FISHING BECOMES A LETHAL SPORT!

Welcome to Minnesota's Annual Lake Winnibigoshish Ice-Caught Fish Chowder-Off.

Ingredients:

- Hamilton Waring - Chairman U.S. Senate Armed Services Committee
- Marvin Maxwell - Chairman U.S. House Armed Services Committee
- Lew Llewellyn - State Governor

They all want to cook the best chowder. They all want to win the White House. And they'll do anything to take both. Anything!

So who will be the next Iced Chef?

PREVIOUSLY PUBLISHED AS DEAD CHEF STORY #1, ICED CHEF!

1

Rikka Albert shouldered the eighty-thousand-dollar Panasonic Varicam video camera, which then tried to freeze to her cheek. It was stupid. They'd designed her beautiful camera to turn the everyday world into television art. Where was *television art* in the middle of a frozen Minnesota lake? Featureless white to the west. And to the north, east, and south just to spite her.

She'd come out a day early to do the pre-shoot planning and all of the B-roll shots before tomorrow's Annual Lake Winnibigoshish Northland Chowder-Off cooking competition—only ice-caught fish allowed.

It was another episode of *Kate's Kitchen Raids* and Rikka was glad to be here. She really was. And if she kept telling herself that often enough, she might actually believe it... someday...like in spring...maybe.

"You people really do this for fun?"

Senator Hamilton Waring, who had nothing to do with blenders but had a lot to do with a massive chunk of iron ore money and being chairman of the US Senate Armed Services Committee, looked completely at home in this sub-

Arctic world. Tall, blond, and broad-shouldered even before he'd hauled on his parka. He looked down at her five-feet of Asian sass as if she was an alien bug.

"I'd say that we Minnesotans are a hardier stock than the rest of the country. We've had to be."

Rikka resisted the urge to point out that driving out onto the ice in a tricked-out crystal-red Cadillac Escalade SUV didn't exactly constitute hardship. The thing looked like a blot of blood in the middle of the winter wonderland. *Try trudging through yet another New York City slush storm and see how you do, Blender-man.* But she kept that thought to herself and looked for something, anything, to focus her camera on.

They were well out on Lake Winnibigoshish. Nearer the shore were numerous fishing shacks set in neat rows. It looked like any small shanty town with street-wide lanes on which SUVs and snowmobiles parked in equal numbers. A line of dark-green pine trees marked the shore, which lay close by the lines of shacks.

But Hamilton Waring had not stopped there. He'd driven almost a mile out onto the ice; ice that shot unnerving snaps and crackles at her like a gun battle in the South Bronx. They'd proceeded north across the sixty-nine thousand acre lake farther and farther from the shore, which she kept eyeing longingly in the passenger side rearview mirror. The tiny words written there—*Objects may be closer than they appear*—made the disappearing shoreline even more achingly distant.

As they drove out, the number of shacks diminished, but their designs became rapidly more elaborate. They passed a lone cute cottage and beyond that, off by themselves, were three ice *shacks* far grander than anything around them. They marked the corners of an empty triangle a hundred feet on a side.

He circled most of the way around one of the shacks before parking in front of a mansion on ice. Like Elsa would have built if all of her capital hadn't been *Frozen.*

It was one of those *tiny houses* that were all the rage, looking like a big house that had shrunk by a few too many runs through high-heat dry cycles. Waring's mini-mansion, in the fake Edwardian, boasted imitation stone siding, numerous bay windows, and a burnished copper roof. The second-story glassed-in cupola—utterly destroying even the most marginal lines of balanced shape—surely offered a commanding view over the vasty nothingness. The thing reeked of money. And an absolute, certifiable lack of taste.

They clambered out of the Cadillac blood blot, but he didn't head for the door. It didn't take Rikka's trained eye to see that he'd been careful in positioning both his SUV and himself. The man knew his camera angles.

What the hell, time to stroke the Senator's ego.

Rikka stepped back, ignoring the gunshot ripple of *ice just adjusting itself a bit* and flipped the camera to record. She started with an opening set-up shot of the lesser shacks clustered in the distance, panned across the sparser, and clearly far richer, neighborhood out here on the offshore ice. Slowed as she passed over one of the two equally ostentatious ice *shacks* next to Waring's—one that boasted Bavarian white walls, dark wood angular trim, and massive porch beams—and finally to the man, his SUV, and his own *humble* shack.

He wore a self-deprecating smile, that was probably meant to express an approachable billionaire who welcomed you to his playpen, but instead said, *I could be your next President and there ain't shit you can do about it.* Man seriously needed an image consultant to kick his ass around the ice a few hundred times. The election was still a ways off, perhaps long enough for a plastic surgeon to surgically remove the overdose of smug.

Bet this clip gets cut. Unless he lost tomorrow's Chowder-Off, then maybe she could slip it in as the before-the-fall shot.

In addition to being handsome, rich, powerful, and totally full of himself, he was also the reigning champion of the Lake Winnibigoshish Annual Northland Chowder-Off —three years running.

"So, Senator, how are you feeling about your chances in tomorrow's competition?" Give him a leading question and maybe he'd drop out of smarmy mode and give her a decent image to use.

"Well, you betcha there are some fine cooks out here on the ice. Congressman Marvin Maxwell is good," he pointed off-screen toward the Bavarian ice house that showed even less taste than Blender-man's if possible. "He uses too much pepper, but don't let on."

"Scout's honor," Rikka prompted him, knowing she could edit out her comment later.

"Over there..." he pointed the other way.

Rikka would have to remember and shoot some footage of the hideous affair to the east. It was white on white on ice. Fake Corinthian columns under a carved portico complete with naked gods and goddesses, all painted in faux marble. It wasn't faux Greek, it was a genuine fake copy of the real faux McCoy Greek. The generational distancing had not been kind to it.

"That's Governor Llewellyn's place. He's placed second to my chowder twice now, so I've got to watch him close."

"Not *enough* pepper?" Rikka guessed.

"Manhattan style," Hamilton said grimly.

"Eww!" Rikka would have to agree with him there. She

was originally from Boston and still cringed every time she saw chowder with a tomato base. It was like pizza with Chow Mein noodles; she liked both, but together?

"My pop's recipe, with a few secret changes of my own, has fended them off so far, and it will again."

"So, we have the top three chowder chefs in the Northland who are also three of the top-seeded men for the next Presidential election, all on the same piece of ice. Quite a coincidence." And if they elected Blender-man, she'd move to another country.

"Not at all, little lady. Not at all."

She'd *little lady* him right in the shins if she wasn't filming this.

"Minnesota breeds more than hardy stock. It breeds great political leaders. But neither one will beat me on the political or the foodie field."

Rikka decided not to point out that *foodie* was a thoroughly passé term. The final tombstone on the word's grave had been the McDonald's ad campaign, *Foodies Welcome!*

"Any non-political combatants?" she asked instead.

"Combatants? We're all friends out here braving the deep ice. That's what we call it out here, farther from shore. The ice is actually thinner, but the water is deeper and the catch better. That's one of the reasons we're always the top three in the Chowder-Off."

Thinner ice? Rikka wished she'd booked her flight to Florida instead, which was really saying something—she hated Florida.

The noble warrior led her forward to the front door of his humble little ice shack. He unlocked the door and held it open for her to enter first. The blissfully warm air washed over her as she entered.

Rikka let the camera be the first-time visitor, first taking in the oak paneling, green-shaded lamps, and deep red leather chairs—all more fit for a brandy-and-cigar political meeting than an ice fishing hovel. A lush oriental rug, that Rikka could see was exceptional work, covered most of the floor.

Close beside each chair, an eighteen-inch hole had been punched through the carpet and covered with a metal and rubber plate. Each chair had its own private ice-fishing hole. She resisted the urge to smack the man for committing such blatant crime-against-carpet as he pointed to various features of his little *home away from home.*

There were two rooms on this level. At this end of the great room housed a fully equipped kitchen and a spiral staircase leading upward to the glass cupola. The middle of the room was the sitting area, which included the finest whiskey bar she'd seen since the G-7 meeting at Inverlochy Castle Hotel in Scotland. The far wall was mostly covered by a massive television screen that stood as tall as she did— though she wasn't complaining because at the moment it was playing a recording of a massive log fire. It made her feel warmer, at least psychologically.

Through the open door to one side was a master bedroom, again with fishing-hole hatches cut through the fine Persian runner rugs.

The hatch cover to the other side of the bed had been raised, exposing the hole in the ice and the dark water lapping only inches below.

Rikka would have felt unnerved all over again that she was standing only a mere foot above forty feet of icy depths, but there was a distraction.

A woman lay on the carpet to one side of the fishing hole. Her parka at her feet. Her skin-tight slacks and form-hugging silk turtleneck advertised that she was a particularly well-endowed one. She might have been relaxing and watching for a fish to tug on her line.

Except for one problem.

Rather than greeting Rikka with a smile of surprise, she had no expression whatsoever.

The voluptuous form lacked one key item—its head.

Long blonde tresses still trailed across the carpet, but the missing body part bobbed in the dark water of the fishing hole.

Rikka recognized Lulu, the wife of Governor Llewellyn, from the prep file—despite her having gone to pieces. Maybe thoughtful, Rikka considered. Perhaps dismayed. It was hard to read the expression literally frozen on her face by the freezing water.

"Well, that's different," was all Rikka could think to say before calling for the Senator to remark on the arrival of his departed guest.

2

"I've really got to talk to Kate about sending me out on these bizarre assignments," Rikka spoke into her phone as she waited for her pizza at Rasley's Blueberry Bowl— "Voted Number One in the Northland, honey!" the overly blonde waitress in the blueberry-shaded uniform had insisted on telling her.

Apparently, *this* was the hot spot of Deer River, Minnesota.

Rikka had considered several sharp ripostes, including a quick left jab, but finally reconsidered. She'd even resisted the verbal right cross of telling the waitress she was from New York where—even if pizza hadn't originated—it had long since been perfected. Atypically, she'd kept her mouth shut.

Which didn't sound like her at all.

She put a hand to her forehead but didn't feel a fever.

Rasley's decorations leaned strongly toward dingy brown. The place echoed with the sharp crack of tumbling bowling pins from the ten lanes heating up behind her. The men of Deer River might be out on the ice, but their wives, with one notable exception, were here and they were in league.

At the other end of the phone call, Sam Fierro didn't respond. He knew that sometimes Rikka just had to process out loud. She'd caught him at his butcher shop, Fierro Meats, in Brooklyn.

Kate Stark was a problem, though.

She'd be Rikka's closest friend, if Rikka believed in friends. The woman was everything Rikka wasn't and she tried not to let it piss her off too often, but at the moment it most certainly did.

Kate was tall with jet-black hair brushing her shoulders and crystalline blue eyes, had a figure to make men weep, and was the billionaire owner of Cooks Network. She also could out-cook most of the people on her shows, which Rikka totally respected her for, and had a wardrobe to die for...none of which would fit Rikka's tiny frame. Yet another reason for a grudge.

"The worst thing Kate is doing to me right now is not being here until tomorrow, and I'm starting to take it personally." Since when did she care about getting someone else's help?

Which didn't sound like her either.

She checked the lymph nodes under her jaw but couldn't detect any swelling. Oddly, she'd begun to rely on Kate, Kate's twin brother Paul, and Sam...especially Sam.

Sam, being a wise man, didn't say anything.

"Well, the situation here is even dumber than I first thought now that Minnesota's First Lady has turned up a foot shorter than usual." Rikka really shouldn't be whining, especially not to someone in a whole different time zone, but he was the only one handy; and the one she'd found she could turn to time and again.

Besides, Kate would be in the middle of the Eric Ripert interview right now, a total fan moment for Kate, and no way was Rikka interrupting that.

Gods!

Since when had she become considerate? Shoot her quick and put her out of her misery. Tomorrow morning would be soon enough when Kate was due in the Gopher State as a principal judge for the Northland Chowder-Off, so Rikka was on her own until then.

"The Governor came right on out," she told Sam, then sipped her glass of Rasley's house red. Major mistake! She edged it as far away across the table as she could. Then she thought better of allowing it to remain so close by and carried the glass over to an as yet uncleared table. She covered it with a napkin, so that it couldn't see her anymore, before retreating to the safety of her own table and continuing.

Thankfully, Sam was one of those great guys who was comfortable with silence in a conversation. Or had grown used to Rikka's peripatetic conversational style.

"Governor Llewellyn beat the coroner-police chief—they're the same person here which tells you how far off the map this place really is—to Waring's Edwardian mini-palace by ramming his car into the Chief's bumper and almost skidding her into the front door of his own Greek Palace fishing shack. I'll send you pictures. First, they were all being too damn polite about, 'I just don't understand how she got here, Lew,' and 'This isn't going to look good to the voters, Ham,' that they never thought about what lay in the room with them. Or rather who."

Sam allowed her to let the suspense build.

"I had my camera running the whole time," Rikka patted it on the recording head, where it perched on the table beside her, because it had been such a good girl. She was sitting quite alone; Rasley's restaurant had emptied when the bowling league games began.

"If Kate wants to break into the news business, I have every moment in hi-def video. They're keeping it hush-hush, so we've got the scoop if we want it."

Sam's pregnant pause spoke volumes.

"I know. I'm jumping the gun, but it's good, Sam. Governor Llewellyn, Police Chief Patrice Smith, Senator Hamilton Waring, and a headless woman; three of them doing a polite two-step like they just ate a whole bushel of green apples and there's only one pot to go in. Though First Lady Lulu Llewellyn didn't do much, part of her just lay there and the other part sort of watched them."

Overly Blonde finally delivered the pepperoni, mushroom, and onion pizza that Rikka had been smelling for far too long. When she started chit-chatting, Rikka continued to Sam over the phone, "It's not every day that a woman's body ends up in one part of your bedroom and her head in another. The blood trail made such interesting patterns."

Overly Blonde evaporated, after turning almost as green as her outfit was blue.

Rikka wasn't about to waste pizza, good or not. She bit down and seared her mouth nicely. Decent sauce. Real cheese. Not New York, but not too shabby. Maybe Minnesota wasn't as awful as her first, second, and third assessments.

Sam held the line while she dragged in some cool air. Then they caught up on the miscellaneous news of the day.

Overly Blonde cleared some tables, including the awful wine that had been watching her from under its napkin, before heading back over for the "Isn't our pizza wonderful?" question.

"The blood," Rikka returned to the former topic on the phone, "was pretty impressive, even if most of it went down the hole. Human body sure contains a lot, doesn't it?"

Rikka made a show of biting into her next piece of pizza as the waitress greened up again and about faced.

"Wait a sec, Sam."

Governor Llewellyn and Senator Hamilton Waring Not-the-blender-man came in, spotted her, and stalked over to her table. Hamilton dropped a coroner's report on her table. She'd seen plenty of these in a past life, back when she was a computer specialist for a Chinese money laundering operation that had fronted for the North Koreans without her knowing it, and spotted the relevant box immediately.

"You're going to love this," she continued to Sam. "The coroner pumped the First Lady's stomach. Her last meal was chowder. It had an exceptionally high ratio of pepper. Something Congressman Marvin Maxwell is known for. Yes," she said before Sam could ask, "the Chairman of the House Armed Services Committee."

Sam would know plenty about both Maxwell and Waring as head of the two Congressional Armed Services committees. He was Marine Force Recon (retired). He'd made it clear early on in their acquaintance that there was no such thing as an ex-Marine.

"Why did you track *me* down?" she asked the two men, as if she and Sam didn't already know. She surreptitiously set her phone to speaker, knowing Sam would keep quiet while he listened.

The Governor didn't look too broken up about the unexpected murder of his wife, but whether that was reality or Minnesota stoicism, Rikka couldn't tell.

"We," Hamilton seemed to be having trouble clearing his throat, "need an impartial witness when we confront Marvin Maxwell so that—" he hesitated again and Rikka finished for him.

"—so that you have proof that there is no bias related to tomorrow's Chowder-Off."

Waring and Llewellyn nodded in unison, like the *Dumb and Dumber* twins.

Sam may have snorted quietly, but Rikka couldn't tell because she was too busy laughing in their faces.

They didn't take it very well.

3

RIKKA AND SENATOR HAMILTON FOUND CONGRESSMAN Marvin Maxwell's wife Marilyn in Lane Four of Rasley's Blueberry Bowl, well on her way to breaking two hundred. Like the dead First Lady of Minnesota, Lulu Llewellyn, she was another tall and fiercely buxom Minnesotan, as proven by her particularly well-tailored bowling shirt that had *Marilyn* stitched over one prominent breast and *Maxwell* over the other.

"Marvin's out on the ice. Said he had wanted a couple more perch for the Chowder-Off. Didn't even come home last night. If I find he was with Lew's wife Lulu, like you always are Hamilton, he just might find himself down an ice hole."

Like the savvy politician he was, Hamilton maintained a straight face as he replied, "I can promise you there's no chance of that, Marilyn."

Right, not with Governor Llewellyn's wife being decapitated at Waring Blender-man's shack and now lying in the morgue.

Marilyn nodded, turned, and rolled her personalized

hot-pink bowling ball to catch the six-ten spare, continuing her scoring streak.

They gathered up the Governor—from where he was chatting up Overly Blonde Waitress lady while she boxed up the rest of Rikka's pizza—before climbing into Senator Waring's blood-blot red SUV.

"Think we oughtta get Patrice in on this as well? Make it all legal?"

"She said she was headed back to the ice. We'll stop by and pick her up. She's one of the few women on the deep ice," Hamilton explained as they drove out into the wintry darkness.

Police Chief Patrice Smith's cabin was by far the least ostentatious shack in the deep-ice neighborhood. A quarter the size of the other behemoths, it looked like a fairy tale cottage with its arched windows, sharply peaked roof, and a fake-brick chimney puffing out smoke from her woodstove.

She climbed aboard and they drove the last several hundred yards to Congressman Marvin Maxwell's Bavarian wonderland.

"Odd that he didn't come out to see all of the excitement earlier."

Patrice's comment had the two men shift plans mid-step, and suddenly Patrice was shuffled to the fore and left to knock.

There was no answer and the door was locked.

She fished out a key ring and the third one opened the door.

"Where did you get Marvin's key?" the Governor asked. "Marvin doesn't give anyone his key."

Patrice grimaced. "I found this key ring in your wife Lulu's pocket, Governor Llewellyn."

"Oh."

They all offered a Minnesota shrug, then Patrice opened the door and went in.

Rikka nosed in her camera close behind the Police Chief.

The Bavarian décor was as complete inside as it was outside. A long polished-wood bar. Shelves lined with beer steins. A half dozen beer taps—which were the only real breaks to the motif as their brands were: Budweiser, Bud Lite, Old Milwaukee, Pabst Blue Ribbon...the only concession to Germany was Michelob Genuine Draft. At least it had a German name, even if they brewed it in Columbus, Ohio.

There was one other break in the overall décor.

The headless body lying over the only open ice fishing hole.

A quick inspection revealed no sign of the missing head, but there was little doubt as to his identity. The decapitated Congressman wore a t-shirt stating *Keep Calm and Draw a Pint.*

4

IT WAS A SEVEN A.M. SUNRISE BY THE TIME CONGRESSMAN Maxwell was all squared away in the morgue and Rikka was wondering just what the purpose of having a hotel room was if she never had a chance to sleep in it. Hopefully her luggage had enjoyed its quiet night.

Patrice had moved the Congressman's body back at her morgue to lie beside the Governor's wife—though his head remained at large. She'd done what she could with her limited facilities, like determining that Marvin had also eaten his own over-peppered chowder as a last meal. That had led to the inevitable question of what else had they shared yesterday.

The men had gone off to bed, but Rikka had accompanied Patrice throughout her investigation, including a return to both crime scenes out on the ice. Rikka had leapt at Patrice's suggestion that she remain in the heated car the second time they went out. Patrice had used the door keys to both Maxwell's and Waring's that she'd found in First Lady Llewellyn's pockets to unlock the doors.

It was sunrise by the time the Secret Service agent

finally showed up. Close behind followed an investigator from Camp Riley National Guard training center—some poor schmuck woken from a long winter's nap after a serious battle with a bottle of vodka—selected because he served at the closest military base in all of Minnesota.

A dead Governor's wife had been a minor police matter.

An equally dead Chairman of the House Armed Services Committee drew high-level concern from Washington.

The race for President was down by one.

No losses in Senator Blender-man's corner yet, except for Lulu being found dead beside his bed.

Kate wasn't due for another couple hours.

Everyone involved had gathered together back out on the chill ice as the weak morning sun tried to do something about the minus ten degree temperature—with no success that Rikka could feel. They stood at the center of the triangle, equidistant from Senator Waring's Edwardian mini-mansion, Congressman Maxwell's Bavarian beer hall, and Governor Llewellyn's Grecian temple.

Were Rikka and her poor camera the only ones freezing to death? Some of these people hadn't even bothered to zip up their parkas.

"We know," Patrice started out, "that Congressman Marvin Maxwell and First Lady Lulu Llewellyn both ate similar chowder recipes shortly before dying."

"Before or after they fornicated like dogs in heat?" Marilyn Maxwell asked as if it was of no real surprise what her husband did—including literally losing his head.

"I can't tell in relation to when they dined, but we did find two condoms in the Congressman's trash. Used ones. And I can't tell much more without a DNA kit, but the deceased First Lady did appear to have had sex recently."

"Twice? More than he ever gave to me in the same week," Marilyn huffed out a breath that instantly fogged and then, Rikka would have to check the recording later, froze and made a miniature snowfall to the ice. It was just that cold. *And you people live here on purpose?*

"Or my wife ever gave me," the Governor didn't look at all pleased.

Senator Waring wisely didn't say anything about what or how often he got anything from the governor's wife before she'd been rude enough to die in his icy bedroom.

Mr. Secret Service looked worried, but hadn't shifted from close by Senator Waring's side. The investigator from the National Guard merely looked hung over.

"Could we go somewhere warmer?" Rikka finally begged after all feeling below her knees went missing.

They all looked at her in surprise.

"Of course," Governor Llewellyn was the first to recover. "We'll go to my place. At least it isn't a crime scene." His look at Senator Blender-man was archly smug. *Didn't any of these people understand the purpose the little red light atop a television camera?* She'd been recording everything, even as she kept it tucked in the crook of her arm.

At the Greek revival's door, complete with little leaded glass windows, the Governor unlocked the deadbolt, and tried to usher Senator Waring in first.

"No, Lew. It's your place. You should lead the way."

The Governor waved Rikka forward, "The photographer..."

Rikka wanted to poke him. First, she was a *videographer* and second, she had a name even if no one in town other than the police chief had yet used it.

"...hasn't seen the inside of *my* little ice shack yet."

Rikka dutifully took the lead as they approached the

Greek colonnade. Her legs felt like useless stumps, but at the promise of imminent warmth, they staggered her forward.

When he pulled open the door for her, Rikka closed her eyes for a moment to enjoy the waft of heat.

Then, remembering what she'd found the last two places she'd been, she swung the camera about while watching carefully through the eyepiece before entering. Nope. No corpses in the Spartan interior. White walls, white marble floors, a glass bar that supported only gin, white rum, and vodka bottles. Even a crystal chandelier for light. Close beside the fishing holes through the floor—which had disconcerting Plexiglas covers so she could see the dark waters below—there were uncomfortable-looking lounge chairs that might have been designed to look like Grecian divans as conceived by a top designer for Walmart.

No bodies, though one of the holes was open.

Someone tugged on the back of her coat just as she took a step forward. It made her hesitate a moment with only the camera lens across the threshold.

Rikka heard a high-pitched zipping sound, like a knife being slipped over a sharpening steel. Then the camera would have jerked from her hands, if she didn't have the strap wrapped around her arm.

Instead, she stumbled ahead toward the open ice hole. She struggled, but it dragged her relentlessly by a thin piece of wire that had been looped loosely on the inside edge of the door frame. It now had her camera lens tightly wrapped in its evil clutches. It looked like the titanium multi-threaded fishing lead that Senator Hamilton Waring had been so proud of: *No perch will bite through that and steal my hook.*

Five feet from the hole, she had an idea.

Three feet, she grabbed onto the lens.

On her knees—twelve inches from her camera being dragged down the fishing hole—she twisted the lens free from the camera body's mount.

With a splash of freezing water in her face, seven thousand dollars of lens disappeared down into the murky depths.

5

Pandemonium broke out around her. At least Rikka assumed this was what a Minnesotan version would look like.

"Someone tried to kill me," the Governor sounded deeply shocked.

Everyone looked about for the criminal, some of them even wandering off to look behind the uncomfortable chair-things.

Police Chief Patrice Smith kept her head. She came over, helped Rikka back to her feet, and handed her a white bar towel to wipe her face.

"Are you okay?"

Now that she was dry and had ascertained that she wasn't being dragged along in darkness beneath the ice...

"As long as I'm warm, I'm fine."

Patrice patted her shoulder and returned her attention to the others who had continued their search of the room yet only discovered the bar. Most of them now had a drink despite the early hour. The National Guardsman was the last to act, decided on the hair of the dog, and knocked back a double shot of vodka with a wince.

Rikka shut down the camera and dug a lens cap out of her pocket to protect the camera until she could fetch another lens from her kit back at the hotel she hadn't slept in.

"Well, at least we now know how the murders were committed," Patrice observed calmly.

They all stared at her in astonishment. The Governor crossed rapidly to the bar for another tot of gin.

"A wire lasso run under the ice from another shack," Rikka provided for those slow on the uptake. "A trap just waiting for someone to enter their fishing shack and trigger it."

The reactions were galvanic and fascinating.

Rikka wished she was still recording; it made for great theater.

The Governor punched Senator Hamilton Waring and broke his pretty nose while screaming, "It's because you want to be President instead of me. You had to kill off my lovely wife to hide your affairs with her. Then you killed poor old Marvin because he has a far better voting record than you. If it hadn't been for the cameraman—"

Videographer woman! Rikka grumbled beneath her breath.

"—you were going to off me to clear your path to the White House. That's why you wanted me to go through the door first."

"Nonsense," Waring warmed up his rebuttal while spattering red blood from his nosebleed all over the pristine white surfaces. "I didn't worry about either of you for a second in the run against me. You wanted to frame me for your wife's death, because she knew what a real man was like. And you killed off poor Marvin so that you could marry Marilyn."

Rikka turned to Marilyn in time to catch the shifting expression of repugnance on her face.

"Dumb choice, Lew," the lady in question offered her vote. "You're even worse in bed than Hamilton is. Don't know what the First Lady ever saw in either of you, or in Marvin, for that matter. Of course, Lulu was never the sharpest thing, poor girl."

Both men sputtered.

Meanwhile, Mr. Secret Service sat on one of the fake-Grecian divans to await results. Odd. He wasn't reacting the way she'd come to expect from the Secret Service agents she'd met over the years. The military investigator made a similar choice to sit. He retained consciousness for several seconds, but no more than that.

Police Chief Patrice Smith watched quietly with her arms crossed.

Finally, the three Minnesotans wound down, not knowing who else to accuse.

Senator Waring's nosebleed was staunched.

The Governor's face no longer glared as red as a runway beacon with high blood pressure.

Marilyn Maxwell looked resigned about her only two choices for getting to the White House. Or maybe at having to find a new set of lovers. Or maybe just wishing them both dead for being such idiots. Perhaps sad that they'd survived the various attacks—that fit too.

Rikka finally had a moment to consider, "How were those wires positioned under the ice, anyway? Do any of you scuba?"

Everyone shook their heads no, except for the National Guardsman, who offered a deeply adenoidal snore.

"And where did my goddamn seven-thousand dollar lens go?"

6

THERE WAS A KNOCK ON THE DOOR.

When it opened, no additional sunlight made it into the room. A large man with broad shoulders filled the doorway. His hair was crew cut and he wore a faded sweatshirt that said *USMC* across the front. His big hands had no gloves despite the bitter cold.

Rikka threw herself at him and he caught her easily.

"Sam!" she kissed him hard. She'd actually thrown herself at a man and kissed him...and meant it. It might not be the Rikka Albert she knew, but she could get to like this woman she was turning into. By the way he kissed her back, Sam certainly appeared to approve.

She dragged him into the Grecian shack's main room and closed out the frigid morning.

It only took moments to fill him in on the events since her pizza call last night.

He'd come for her. For HER! Rikka checked in with herself and about her most coherent thought was, *Wow!*

He moved forward silently to the ice hole where her lens had disappeared—he was so light of foot you couldn't even

31

hear his boots on the faux-marble floor. Yet he moved with such determination that everyone scrambled to get out of his way.

Kneeling, he stared at the hole for a long moment. She could see his Marine Force Recon mind working. These were the guys sent in behind enemy lines and told to *figure it out*. In for twenty years, Sam had been one of their very best. After mere seconds, he reached down into the icy water as if it was a warm bath and swirled his hand around the lower edge.

"Of course!" Rikka then explained to the others over her shoulder, knowing they wouldn't get it. "There would be a groove cut in the bottom lip of the ice by the wire running in the direction it was being pulled from."

Sam pointed in the direction her lens had gone.

Rikka latched onto Sam's arm as he led the way. She was so glad to see him she was feeling all bubbly and chirpy and...and...girly, she decided. Weird!

Maybe it was okay to feel that around him.

But only him. She had standards to maintain.

Sam led them directly to Senator Waring's Edwardian mini-palace of a fish shack. Patrice unlocked the heavy deadbolt for them.

There, in the middle of the living room, was an open fishing hole cover. Beside it, a heavy-duty fishing reel with a motorized winding spool was attached to a small stand. Her lens dangled in its villainous noose.

"Where did that come from?" Waring protested, but no one believed him. It certainly hadn't been there last night when she and Patrice had returned to the scene or they would have noticed it.

Rikka retrieved her lens and tested it. It seemed none

the worse for its dunking after she'd dried it off with a plush maroon towel that matched the leather furniture.

There was a sharp snap of handcuffs. Patrice had latched Senator Waring to the circular staircase leading up to his eagle's aerie lounge. "I hereby arrest you for the attempted murder of Governor Llewellyn."

He sputtered and protested as she read him his rights.

Meanwhile, Rikka led Sam to the hole where the Governor's wife was decapitated.

The wire-notch goose chase then led them to Congressman Marvin Maxwell's cabin. That meant that Marvin had set the trap in Senator Waring's bedroom that had killed the Governor's wife shortly after he'd slept with her.

It didn't take much digging around among the beer kegs behind the bar to unearth another powered spool.

"The Congressman," Patrice inspected it carefully, "must have hidden this away after he killed First Lady Llewellyn, but before he was, in turn, killed. Yes," she held up the end of the wire. "There are several long blonde hairs still wound around the wire. No one on the deep ice but the First Lady has hair this long."

Marilyn Maxwell's was shoulder length and Patrice's was even shorter.

Rikka also found a fancy looking remote control with two tiny joysticks, "It's like those things to radio-control those toy drones."

Sam had continued his search. Behind a keg of Bud Lite, he unearthed a small submarine as long as Rikka's forearm.

"I," everyone turned to look at Marilyn—except for the military security guy they'd left asleep in the Governor's shack and Senator Hamilton Waring who remained shackled to the staircase of his own fish shack for safe keeping. "I gave each of the boys one of those last summer. Three remote-controlled submarines that they could have mock battles with on the lake."

"I remember that," Patrice was nodding.

"They must have used them to carry a lead under the ice and each set up a trap," Rikka tried to think it through. "First, Congressman Maxwell must have tried to murder Senator Waring. But he killed poor First Lady Lulu Llewellyn instead when she entered the Senator's bedroom."

"Then someone decapitated poor Marvin." Marilyn shook her head though she didn't appear too sad about the loss.

"And just now," Patrice picked up the line of logic, "Senator Waring tried to kill Governor Llewellyn, but by pure chance caught your camera lens instead."

Sam didn't even need to point to the hole where Congressman Marvin Maxwell had died for Rikka to know the next question.

"Now, let's find out where Marvin's head has gone."

One last time, her Sam—*her Sam, she kind of liked the way that sounded*—plunged his hand into the icy depths. She found him a Bavarian-brown towel to dry his hand with as he rose to his feet and slowly turned to face Governor Llewellyn.

They left Maxwell's Bavarian beer hall and crossed the ice once more to Llewellyn's Greek temple, completing the sides of the triangle. Back in the Governor's palace of white, in an open fishing hole close beside the claw-foot bathtub—white, of course—dangled Marvin Maxwell's head caught in a loop of wire.

"It seems," Chief Patrice Smith noted in a dry voice, "that the Governor didn't want any competition for his run at the White House either. After all, he'd know that only forty percent of our Presidents were governors first. His chances against both Maxwell and Waring would have been poor. He had to level the playing field."

"I would never—"

The Secret Service agent ignored the Governor's protests as he cuffed him to the clawfoot tub.

"They'll have to go to trial for—" Patrice started, but the not-so Secret Service man cut her off.

His look of disgust gave him away.

Rikka knew from experience that the US Secret Service would never reveal any judgment about the people they protected. Well, if he wasn't Secret Service...

"We are not going to have the two Chairmen of the Congressional and Senate Armed Services Committees and a dirty Governor besmirching the news nor the next Presidential election with their petty rivalries. Now if you would all kindly leave." He sounded more like a special troubleshooter for a political party—perhaps the one that all three men had shared.

He rousted the military man and sent him stumbling out to return to his base.

The troubleshooter sounded dangerous and borderline psychotic.

Rikka checked in with Sam.

Sam and the troubleshooter squared off and eyed each other for a long moment. No question Sam would win if it came down to a fight, but she also knew that no one loved his country more than Sam. Getting his hands dirty in its name was not a foreign concept to a Marine Force Recon soldier, retired or not.

Though it was a long time coming, his slight nod of

agreement was enough for her. If Sam thought it was best to stay out of this guy's way, she wouldn't argue.

Kate was going to hate this, but Rikka shut down the camera and pulled out the memory card. Then she reached into her boot and pulled out the second copy she'd made as they came back out on the ice this morning, and handed them both to the agent.

Patrice drove Marilyn, Sam, and Rikka back to Patrice's ice shack, where she made them all freshly brewed coffee. It was as cozy and feminine inside as it was cute outside. The Police Chief had faced her shack so that the three ridiculous buildings grouped at the outer edge of safety didn't pollute her view. Instead, the windows faced the distant shore and the sun climbing above the dark tree line.

Rikka more felt than heard the heavy *thump* behind her. This ice beneath Patrice's shack groaned in protest but soon settled.

By unspoken agreement, they waited.

The not-so-much-a-Secret Service-agent's vehicle passed by on its way to clear out the morgue and Patrice's coroner files.

They finished their coffee, enjoying the leisurely three-way conversation. Sam didn't say much, just keeping her close on the couch beside him.

After lunch, they went outside to look at the empty horizon to the north across Lake Winnibigoshish.

No three fishing shacks. No blood-blot red Cadillac SUV. No three men at war over the Presidency of the United States by whatever means necessary.

Something had broken the ice. Perhaps the papers would attribute it to the excess weight of the extravagant fish-shack palaces and massive SUVs out on the deep ice.

Whatever the actual cause, everything had disappeared

from view. By tonight, the ice would refreeze over the shattered chunks that now filled that area of the lake. In a week, it would be walkable. A team of special divers would surely be called, but a thorough investigation would have to wait until spring and melt-out.

Patrice and Marilyn went back inside to prepare for the Lake Winnibigoshish Northland Chowder-Off this afternoon.

Sam drove Rikka to go pick up Kate.

7

"You know," Kate Stark sat back in her chair after tasting the four dozen chowders entered in the contest, "that's quite some story, Rikka."

"I know. I almost didn't tell you, but Sam thought you'd like to know." She'd filled Kate in on all of the details she could remember while the chowders had been cooking on portable stoves, in between when Kate had wandered from chef to chef for *on-the-ice* interviews.

The Chowder-Off was a near-shore event, with a section of the ice polished for an ice skating rink, Genuine Lake Winnibigoshish Ice snow cones, and a fairway of game booths and crafts. Everyone had bundled up in heavy parkas—though a good third were unzipped—making merry of the sunny day that had reached a balmy ten degrees above zero.

"By the way, Kate, I'm putting in for an equatorial assignment next time."

Kate laughed in that way that wished Rikka good luck. "Odd that all three men thought to use the same method," she said with little change of tone.

"Maybe one thought it up, told it as a joke to the others, and then they each decided to give it a go."

"Could be," Kate admitted and started flipping through her scoring notes again. "Could be." She began handing losers to Rikka.

Rikka read the tasting notes and was once again awed by Kate. There were nuances and subtleties marked down that Rikka didn't even know about, never mind stood a chance of noticing.

For her, there was one pretty clear winner, but maybe she was biased.

Kate finally winnowed the stack down to the top three and flicked one of her perfectly manicured but unpainted nails against the winner. Well, Rikka was pleased to have been right about that.

"Maybe," Kate said quietly as the crowds gathered to hear the final judging and prize awards, "a fourth person suggested it to each of them individually. Though there's no way to tell who now."

Rikka blinked at that, then Kate gave her a nudge toward a good camera position as she moved to the carved ice podium and prepared to speak. Rikka got the camera aimed and gave her friend a nod that she was recording.

Kate was funny, of course, and charming. There was a reason the woman ran the Number One food network on television, with the most popular shows being the ones she did herself.

A fourth person, Rikka considered.

Marilyn Maxwell, the dead-Congressman's wife, had given each of the *boys* one of the toy submarines.

And slept with each one, though clearly not as freely as the Governor's wife had. Perhaps only once or twice, to suggest the idea of the trap.

Kate awarded third place amid a large round of cheers and applause.

Rikka tracked a great bearded man in her viewscreen. He was on the verge of weeping with joy as he lumbered forward and wrapped Kate in a great hug that drew laughter and more applause from the audience.

But what would make all three men set their traps on the same day? Perhaps because of it being the day before the Chowder-Off? It still didn't sound right.

What if Marilyn had slept with each merely in order to convince the men to give her a key so that she'd have access to each of their cabins?

Kate called up the second place winner. A tiny elderly woman came trotting forward with her gray braids flapping about her. A clear fan favorite, she also garnered enough heartfelt applause that Rikka feel more kindly toward Minnesota than she had since reading the first weather report when given this assignment.

And then Rikka remembered one fact she hadn't thought to tell Kate.

Who had tugged on the back of her coat and stopped Rikka from sticking her neck into the trap set at the Governor's shack?

No one had admitted to it, but only one person had come to check on her after she'd sprung the trap and lost her lens down an ice hole.

She swung the camera to locate her as Kate called out the winner.

There was a roar of approval as the name was announced.

Her camera caught Police Chief Patrice Smith's radiant smile, the first Rikka had ever seen cross her steadfast-Minnesotan features. And the look bloomed further a moment later when Marilyn Maxwell threw herself into the victor's arms and kissed her soundly.

Rikka captured their moment—one that she'd edit out later and perhaps send to them privately—then panned into the cheering crowd capturing some great footage for the television show.

Rikka herself wouldn't miss the three men from the upcoming Presidential race and she doubted if Patrice or Marilyn would miss them in the years to come.

Patrice Smith, who—Rikka finally recalled from her prep work—had placed a consistent fourth over the years, came to the podium to collect her First Place prize for the best Ice-Caught Fish Chowder. She'd never tasted their chowders, perhaps they'd won on their reputations as major politicians. With them gone, they now had a real winner.

And the cheering continued as the cooks and fans of the Annual Lake Winnibigoshish Northland Chowder-Off proved that they weren't going to miss the three men either.

AFTERWORD

If you enjoyed Iced Chef
please consider leaving a review.
They really help.

Keep reading for an exciting excerpt from:
Kate Stark #1, Final Taste

A list of characters and locations may be found at:
https://mlbuchman.com/people-places-planes#KS

IF YOU ENJOYED THAT,
YOU'LL LOVE...

FINAL TASTE (EXCERPT)

MARIANNE RIMALDI SCOOPED A SCANT TEASPOON OF THE Grand Marnier chocolate ganache and drizzled it atop the single bite of chocolate truffle cheesecake. The perfect final bite for the meal she was creating.

A glance at the competition clock.

Two minutes.

She plated three more desserts for the judges. The television cameras filming *Kate's Kitchen from Hell* hovered close by—two on her, two on her competitor as the final seconds ticked away. One glass-eyed lens had an angle that showed her the cameraman wasn't focused only on the food.

Precisely according to plan.

Marianne needed victory on America's most popular cooking show, which meant winning over at least two judges. More than that, she lusted after *Kate's Kitchen* "Blazing Knife" stamp of approval on her career, which required all three judges' nod of approval on all three courses.

She'd made it through the five runoff contest episodes,

one by the skin of her teeth. But now in the final? Winning was *not* enough. She lusted after that three-vote knife and the prestige that it came sheathed in. For a shot at that, she applied other...ingredients.

The heat of the competition kitchen—the flaring burners and blinding stage lights—simply *forced* her to pull at the cross-shoulder buttons of her confining chef's jacket, which now hung half open. She wore a loose-necked satin blouse beneath, no bra. She'd chosen an emerald green to contrast with the fire-red of the winner's jacket that she intended to be hers at the end of the show. It also stood out well against her unadorned ash-black jacket of a contestant, but she wanted the red.

However, mere party tricks wouldn't work on the show's main judge.

Marianne had to capture Kate Stark's approval. With her, nothing counted except the food itself.

Kate Stark, the blue-eyed, black-haired goddess of television food on the nation's most popular cooking network. She'd founded the show and served as its perennial judge. Always front and center on the panel. That she also owned the entire network only added to her aura of ultimate power.

Deep inside Marianne didn't want to merely win Stark's vote, she wanted to impress the hell out of her. She'd sell her soul to the Devil if needs be; this was *Kate's Kitchen from Hell* after all.

Don't think! Focus on the food...but don't forget the theater.

Marianne's slight build made the least view down her blouse a revealing one. Bent over her dessert plates, the satin draped away from her body allowing a deliciously cool ripple of fresh air to course along her front. Her build might be far less substantial than the one that had made Mom such a success on the *wrong* side of Hollywood, but she'd certainly watched her mom and learned what sold. It had been an educational upbringing, if not a typical one.

Three judges.

Two of them were easy.

Zania, the guest taster, sat in the role of the *every-person's* palate so necessary for engaging an audience. She gave the viewers someone to identify with, among the professional chefs. Of course, her palate was the only thing on Zania *not* extraordinary.

She was the hottest new Hollywood starlet—who Marianne suspected to be a closet butch. It wasn't too dangerous a bet because Zania's mother worked the same side of Hollywood as Marianne's and word got around about what truly happened after the bedding was rumpled in erotic film.

During her intro, Tinsel Town's hot new box-office draw had announced she was centerfolding for *Playboy* next month in the same sultry breath as promoting her new tight-leather, sci-fi thriller movie. Marianne knew that anyone who pegged Zania as an airhead had a nasty surprise coming; she absolutely knew how to market herself. In every way.

However, hints to the actress of possible woman-on-woman bonding that would allow Zania to prove exactly who was the *ultimate female among women* offered definite possibilities for leveraging the star's vote. It looked as if she'd bought into Marianne's careful seasoning of her performance with hints and suggestions.

Marianne's own tastes, however, were for the second guest judge; the professional chef.

Harold Merritt, with his Michelin-starred *Chicago's Merritt* restaurant, was both distinctly handsome and notoriously single. Win or lose, she'd make a point of chatting him up after the show. That broad chest and short dark crewcut gave him a deliciously tough look; she could find many uses for him outside the kitchen, or in it—two bodies, a touch of olive oil, or maybe chocolate sauce...

A careful peek from behind the screen of the jet-black dyed bangs of her blonde hair revealed both Zania and Harold's attention remained fixated on the monitors of the show's live feed rather than gazing benignly over the competition kitchen floor. Their attention remained precisely where Marianne wanted it. On her.

Kate Stark posed a different problem.

The Number One slotted television chef on any network, not merely the one she owned—also watched the monitor, but with a slightly amused smile that Marianne would pay good money to understand. Kate's startling blue eyes, aquiline nose, and straight black hair brushing her shoulders and framing those well-defined cheekbones, also made her one of the most attractive faces on television, cooking or not.

She was a notoriously deadpan judge, at least on this show, so that wry smile must mean something.

For good or ill, Marianne would not find the answer on this side of the judge's table.

The camera judiciously, or injudiciously, spying down her jacket, pulled back, ready to seek another shot. To maximize her own airtime over the competition, Marianne *accidentally* dribbled a large dollop of the orange-chocolate ganache onto the back of her hand. She licked it clean as if too hurried to wipe it away, making sure the camera could see the pleasure on her face at the success of her own work. The guy behind the lens stayed focused on her.

Damn! She'd nailed the ganache. Marianne would win

on taste alone. But she'd have to play the meal presentation carefully, spiking the odds even further in her favor with both of the two guest judges.

The competition buzzer sounded as she shaved the last of the zest of a blood orange using a nutmeg rasp. Even as Marianne held up her hands to show she was done, the camera focused in on the cloud of orange dust, sprinkling through the air like snowflakes.

Her shiny dark green satin blouse made a perfect backdrop, which had *somehow* slipped out of another button. Somehow…because she'd enlarged the buttonhole last night to ensure that it popped free when she raised her arms.

Nailed it.

She had to close her eyes for a moment to steady herself.

Light-headed.

She needed to eat.

Her normal technique of shrugging it off didn't work. Even lowering her arms and subtly bracing herself against the table didn't help clear her head.

Her hands were shaking.

Her hands never shook.

––––––––

Franco Lamar cursed.

The damned bitch wasn't supposed to taste her own food, at least not that big teasing lick off the back of her hand. A small taste and she'd have been fine. For a while. Long enough.

From where he stood, he could see Marianne Rimaldi wavering. He and his men lurked in the shadows of the television studio, far behind the judges' table and well clear of any camera's eye.

Bitch pissed him off.

He held his breath, keeping his men in place. He had a Plan B, but he hated when that happened. Especially because he didn't have a Plan C.

Rimaldi made it through the male competitor's meal service by clutching the edge of her worktable, rousing herself to high-five her sous chef, but not much else.

The studio emptied. Last shoot of the day. Competitor headed for the bathroom after the judges finished critiquing his lame ass. Already a given he'd be going down after that review—not a flicker of emotion from the head judge.

The main kitchen staff and cameramen drifted out precisely as Franco hoped.

Now the room held three judges, two cameramen, one floor director, and dumb bitch Rimaldi.

When she served, the ohs and ahs and cheerful commentary among the sappy judges bolstered her reserves.

Franco could feel his fingers digging into his opposite arms where they were crossed. He always hated this part the most.

In Marine Force Recon, they'd parachute behind enemy lines, observe, assess, and report. They could be weeks on the ground playing cat-and-mouse games with enemy security and military forces. That was fine. Even lying low between Command's final *Go!* and the actual zero-hour start of the operation never bothered him. Find a willing local female, or an unwilling one, and lay her low until it came time for the shit to hit the fan.

The gap between the actual start of an operation and the

launch of his own role in it? He utterly despised that mandated inaction.

Full lock-and-load, then sit on his ass? It had sucked in Recon. It sucked now.

Rimaldi wavered again...but kept going. Tough broad. Her body was shutting down on her and she'd have no idea why. Her brain was going, which meant she'd be past caring.

C'mon bitch. Hold it together long enough to deliver the dessert clean.

She nearly dumped the final plates to the studio's cement floor, earning gasps of surprise from the judges and cameramen that they'd have to edit out.

But she recovered and made it to the table.

Franco held his breath as she stumbled through her presentation. The drug was allowing so little oxygen to her brain that he couldn't believe she remained upright.

Delivered.

Now the tasting.

C'mon, judges.

The movie star wench did even better than he could have hoped.

She ate the poisoned dessert in two neat bites. Then the stupid whore picked up her plate to lick up the puddled chocolate sauce with a long, sensuous move that sent a shiver up his balls.

Licking that plate clean, in addition to the dessert itself? No longer a knockout drug—now a major overdose.

She didn't even wobble. Instead, she collapsed forward, face onto the plate.

Shit!

The actress hit the table so hard that one of her awesomely impressive breasts—only marginally contained in her sheer top—popped free.

Franco looked at the other two judges as the studio exploded in panic.

Kate Stark's hand rested on the male judge's arm to keep him from eating.

The two primary targets both sat there—undrugged.

Rimaldi's body finally figured out that it was already dead, and the chef collapsed to the floor.

That put paid on the two secondary targets: Rimaldi and Zania were past recovery.

Stark and the guy sat there unmoving.

Franco nodded to Jason.

Jason Mann pulled out a dart gun and shot them both in the back of the neck.

They each flinched in turn, then slumped in their seats.

Franco signaled his men to move in. When the studio lights blacked out, the four of them pulled down the night-vision goggles perched on their foreheads. The studio was now visible in a hundred shadings of green.

They pulled the darts out of Kate Stark and Harold Merritt and dragged them back.

Jason stopped to grope Zania's errant breast. He looked ready to do more until Franco hissed at him to get moving.

Their timing must be perfect for this to work, or Plan B would be a worse bust than Plan A.

Down the elevator that their inside man had locked in place for them.

Along the basement corridor.

The moment the hired truck backed against the loading dock; Vince used bolt cutters to cut off the diplomatic-pouch door seal on the empty shipping container. Manuel held the door open as they dropped the two bodies on the mattress inside and Jason injected them with the antidote.

Doors closed, a new seal slapped on—identical to even

the registration number—crimped into place, and Nicky shooed the truck driver on his way in under fifteen seconds.

They dumped their gear into a couple of lawyer's briefcases, and each took a different route to the parking garage.

The container and its cargo were on their way.

They were done and damn well paid.

————

Keep reading direct from the author or at fine retailers everywhere.
Final Taste

ABOUT THE AUTHOR

USA Today and Amazon #1 Bestseller M. L. "Matt" Buchman started writing on a flight south from Japan to ride his bicycle across the Australian Outback. Just part of a solo around-the-world trip that ultimately launched his writing career.

From the very beginning, his powerful female heroines insisted on putting character first, *then* a great adventure. He's since written over 75 action-adventure thrillers and military romantic suspense novels. And more than 200 short stories, and a fast-growing pile of read-by-author audiobooks.

PW declares of his Miranda Chase action-adventure thrillers: "Tom Clancy fans open to a strong female lead will clamor for more." About his military romantic thrillers: "Like Robert Ludlum and Nora Roberts had a book baby."

His fans say: "I want more now...of everything!" That his characters are even more insistent than his fans is a hoot.

As a 30-year project manager with a geophysics degree who has designed and built houses, flown and jumped out of planes, and solo-sailed a 50' ketch, he is awed by what is possible. He and his wife presently live on the North Shore of Massachusetts. More at: www.mlbuchman.com.

Other works by M. L. Buchman: *(* - also in audio)*

Action-Adventure Thrillers

Kate Stark
Final Taste
Ice Burn
Knife's Edge

Miranda Chase
Drone*
Thunderbolt*
Condor*
Ghostrider*
Raider*
Chinook*
Havoc*
White Top*
Start the Chase*
Lightning*
Skibird*
Nightwatch*
Osprey*
Gryphon*
Wedgetail*

Science Fiction / Fantasy

Deities Anonymous
Cookbook from Hell: Reheated
Saviors 101

Contemporary Romance

Eagle Cove
Return to Eagle Cove
Recipe for Eagle Cove
Longing for Eagle Cove
Keepsake for Eagle Cove

Love Abroad
Heart of the Cotswolds: England
Path of Love: Cinque Terre, Italy

Where Dreams
Where Dreams are Born
Where Dreams Reside
Where Dreams Are of Christmas*
Where Dreams Unfold
Where Dreams Are Written
Where Dreams Continue

Non-Fiction

Strategies for Success
Managing Your Inner Artist/Writer
Estate Planning for Authors*
Character Voice
Narrate and Record Your Own
Audiobook*
Beyond Prince Charming: One Guy's
Guide to Writing Men in Romance

Short Story Series by M. L. Buchman:

Action-Adventure Thrillers

Kate Stark
Miranda Chase Stories

Romantic Suspense

Antarctic Ice Fliers
US Coast Guard

Contemporary Romance

Eagle Cove

Other

Deities Anonymous (fantasy)
Single Titles

The Emily Beale Universe
(military romantic suspense)

The Night Stalkers
MAIN FLIGHT
The Night Is Mine
I Own the Dawn
Wait Until Dark
Take Over at Midnight
Light Up the Night
Bring On the Dusk
By Break of Day
Target of the Heart
Target Lock on Love
Target of Mine
Target of One's Own
NIGHT STALKERS HOLIDAYS
Daniel's Christmas*
Frank's Independence Day*
Peter's Christmas*
Christmas at Steel Beach
Zachary's Christmas*
Roy's Independence Day*
Damien's Christmas*
Christmas at Peleliu Cove

Henderson's Ranch
Nathan's Big Sky*
Big Sky, Loyal Heart*
Big Sky Dog Whisperer*
Tales of Henderson's Ranch*

Shadow Force: Psi
At the Slightest Sound*
At the Quietest Word*
At the Merest Glance*
At the Clearest Sensation*

White House Protection Force
Off the Leash*
On Your Mark*
In the Weeds*

Firehawks
Pure Heat
Full Blaze
Hot Point*
Flash of Fire*
Wild Fire
SMOKEJUMPERS
Wildfire at Dawn*
Wildfire at Larch Creek*
Wildfire on the Skagit*

Delta Force
Target Engaged*
Heart Strike*
Wild Justice*
Midnight Trust*

Night Stalkers Reload
Guard the East Flank*

Emily Beale Universe Short Story Series
The Night Stalkers
The Night Stalkers Stories
The Night Stalkers CSAR
The Night Stalkers Wedding Stories
The Future Night Stalkers

Delta Force
Th Delta Force Shooters
The Delta Force Warriors

Firehawks
The Firehawks Lookouts
The Firehawks Hotshots
The Firebirds

White House Protection Force
Stories

Future Night Stalkers
Stories (Science Fiction)

SIGN UP FOR M. L. BUCHMAN'S NEWSLETTER TODAY